UNDINE

UNDINE

FRIEDRICH DE LA MOTTE FOUQUÉE, MARY MACGREGOR

ISBN: 978-93-5344-401-3

First Published: -

LECTOR HOUSE LLP
E-MAIL: lectorpublishing@gmail.com

ON THE THRESHOLD STOOD A LITTLE MAIDEN. SEE PAGE 14.

FRIEDRICH DE LA MOTTE FOUQUÉE

UNDINE

TOLD TO THE CHILDREN BY

MARY MACGREGOR

WITH PICTURES BY
KATHARINE CAMERON

**TO
MARGARET**

ABOUT THIS BOOK

Undine is the name of the water maiden whose story you will read as you turn the leaves of this little book.

Undine is beautiful as the dawn stealing across the waters, beautiful as the spray of the crystal waves.

Yet when she comes to earth she comes to seek for that without which her beauty will be for ever cold, cold and chill as the surge of the salt, salt sea.

Look deep into her blue eyes and you will see why her beauty is so cold, so chill.

In the eyes of every mortal you may see a soul. In the gay blue eyes of Undine, look you long and never so deep, no soul will look forth to meet your gaze.

Love, joy, sorrow, these are the pearls that shine in the eyes of every mortal. But in the eyes of the water maiden there is no gleam of love, no sparkle of joy, no tear of sorrow.

Undine has come to earth to seek for a soul. Without one she may never know the golden gifts God has given to each mortal, gifts these of love, joy, sorrow.

You will read in this little book how Undine, the water maiden, won for herself a human soul.

MARY MACGREGOR.

CONTENTS

LIST OF ILLUSTRATIONS

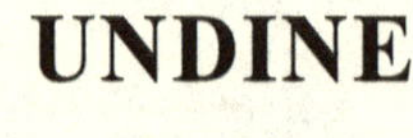

UNDINE

CHAPTER I

THE FISHERMAN AND THE KNIGHT

A fisherman brought a stool to the doorway of his home and, sitting down, he began to mend his nets.

His cottage stood in the midst of green meadows, and his eyes grew glad as he looked at the green grass. After the heat of the fair summer's day it was so cool, so refreshing.

At the foot of the meadows lay a large lake of clear blue water. The fisherman knew it well. It was there his work was done, through sunshine or through storm.

To-day, as his gaze wandered from the green meadows to the blue lake, he thought he saw the waters stretch out soft arms, until slowly they drew the fair meadows, the little cottage into a loving embrace.

The fisherman, his wife and their foster-child lived very quietly on this pleasant spot. It was but seldom that any one passed their door, for between the beautiful meadows and the nearest town lay a wood. So wild and gloomy was the wood, so tangled its pathway, that no one cared to enter it.

Moreover, it was said that there were strange beings lurking amid the gloom — ugly goblins, misshapen gnomes; and there were shadowy spirits too, which flitted through the branches of the strongest trees, and these even the bravest would not wish to see.

Through this dark and haunted wood the old fisherman had often to journey.

It was true that he entered the dreaded shades with fear, yet no spectre ever crossed his path. But perhaps that was because the thoughts of the old man were pure, or perhaps because he never entered the forest without singing a hymn in a clear brave voice.

As the fisherman sat mending his nets on this fair summer eve he began to move restlessly, to glance around uneasily.

Then a sudden terror fell upon him as he heard a noise in the forest behind.

Ah, how the trees rustled and how the grass was being trampled underfoot! Could it be a horseman who made haste to escape from some terrible foe?

And now, although he was wide awake, the fisherman seemed to see a figure, which he had seen before only in his dreams.

He saw the figure of a tall, strong, snow-white man, who came with slow steps toward him, and at each step he took, the figure nodded his great white head.

The fisherman rubbed his eyes as he glanced toward the wood. At the same moment the wind seemed to blow the leaves aside to make room for the snow-white man, whose head never ceased to nod.

'Well,' said the fisherman to himself, 'I have ever passed through the forest unharmed, why should I fear that evil will befall me here?' and he began to repeat aloud a verse of the Bible.

At the sound of his own voice courage crept back into the heart of the fisherman, moreover the words of the Holy Book rebuked his fears. Nor was it long before he was able even to laugh and to see how foolish he had been.

For listen! The white nodding man was after all only a stream which the fisherman knew very well, a stream which ran and bubbled out of the forest and fell into the lake. As for the rustling noise, the fisherman saw what had caused that, as a gaily clad knight rode forth from the forest shadows toward the little cottage.

This was no spectre or spirit of the wood, this stranger who wore the garments of a knight of high degree. He rode a white horse, which stepped softly, so that the flowers in the meadows lifted their delicate heads uninjured by his tread.

The fisherman raised his cap as the stranger drew near, and then quietly went on mending his nets.

Now when the knight saw the old man's face it was welcome to him, as indeed any human face would have been after the terrors of the forest. There he had seen strange mocking faces peering at him whichever way he turned, there he had been followed by strange shadowy forms from which escape had been wellnigh impossible; here at length was a kind and friendly mortal. He would ask him for the food and shelter of which both he and his steed stood in need.

'Dear sir,' answered the fisherman when he had listened to the knight's request, 'dear sir, if you will deign to enter our lonely cottage, you will find a welcome with the food and shelter we offer. As for your horse, can it have a better stable than this tree-shaded meadow, or more delicious fodder than this green grass?'

Well pleased with this answer, the knight dismounted, and together he and the fisherman freed the white horse from its saddle and bridle, and turned it loose into the waving meadow.

Then the old man led the stranger into the cottage.

Here, by the light of the kitchen fire, sat the fisherman's wife. She rose, with a kind greeting for the unexpected guest. Then seating herself again in her armchair, she pointed to an old stool with a broken leg. 'Sit there, good knight,' she said; 'only you must sit still, lest the broken leg prove too weak to bear you.'

Carrying the stool over beside the old woman, the knight placed it carefully on the floor and seated himself as he was bidden. As he sat there talking with the good old fisherman and his wife, it seemed to him almost as though he were their son, who had come home again after journeying in a distant land.

It was only when the knight began to speak of the wood that the fisherman grew restless and refused to listen.

'It were wiser, Sir Knight,' he said, 'not to talk of the wood at nightfall, or indeed to say much of it at any time.'

And then the old couple told their guest how simply they lived in the little cottage by the lake, and they in their turn listened eagerly while the knight told them of himself. He was named Sir Huldbrand, and he dwelt in his castle of Ringstetten, which stood near the source of the river Danube.

Now, as he talked or listened to the quiet tales of the old fisherman, the knight heard a strange sound that seemed to come from the direction of the window. Again and again it came, a strange sound as of water being dashed against the window-panes.

It was plain that the fisherman heard it too, for at each splash a frown crossed his good-natured face.

A louder splash, and a shower of water streamed through the loosely built window-frame into the kitchen.

Then the old man could sit still no longer. He hastened to the window, and opening it called out in an angry voice, 'Undine, cease these childish tricks. A stranger, and he a knight, is in our cottage.'

A low laugh answered him. Hearing it, the old man shut the window and sat down again, saying to his guest, 'Sir Knight, forgive this rude behaviour. Undine my foster-daughter is still only a child, although she is now nearly eighteen years of age. Yet her tricks are harmless, and she herself is full of kindness.'

'Ah,' said the old woman to her husband, 'to you, who are not with her save when the day's work is over, her pranks may seem harmless. But you would not talk so lightly of her ways were she by your side all day. Ever I must watch her, lest she spoil my baking, or undo my spinning or burn the soup. Nay—'

'It is true,' said the old man, interrupting his wife with a smile, 'it is true that you have the maiden by your side throughout the livelong day, while I have but the sea. Yet when the sea is rough and breaks down my dykes I do not love it the less. Even so do you love the little one no less for all her tricks and tiresome ways.'

The old woman turned to her guest. 'Indeed, Sir Knight, he speaks truly. It is not possible to be angry with the maiden long.'

At that moment the door flew open, and she, the maiden of whom they spoke, entered the little kitchen. She was fairer far than any one the knight had ever seen.

'Father,' she cried, 'where is he, the stranger guest?'

Even as she spoke her eyes fell on the knight, who had sprung to his feet as she entered the cottage. He stood gazing in wonder at the marvellous beauty of the maiden.

But before he could greet her, she was at his side, trustingly looking up into his face. Then kneeling before him, she seized his hand and made him seat himself again on the broken old stool.

'You are beautiful, Sir Knight,' she said, 'but how did you come to this little cottage? Have you looked for us long before you could find us? Have you had to pass through the terrible forest ere you could reach us, Sir Knight?'

The knight would have told the maiden the story of his adventures in the wood, but Undine's foster-mother was already speaking, and her tones were loud and angry.

'Go, maiden, go get you to work, and trouble not the stranger with your questions.'

Then Undine, unashamed, drew a little footstool near to Huldbrand, and sitting down to her spinning, cried, 'I shall work here, close to the beautiful knight.'

The old fisherman took no notice of the wilful maiden, and began to speak of other things, hoping that the guest would forget his foster-daughter's questions.

But even had the knight been able to forget, Undine did not mean to sit there quietly, her questions unanswered.

Her sweet voice broke upon the silence. 'Our beautiful guest has not yet told me how he reached our cottage,' she said.

'It is even as you thought,' answered the knight. 'I journeyed through the haunted wood ere I found this safe and hospitable shelter.'

'Then tell me of your wonderful adventures,' demanded the maiden, 'for without these no one may pass through the forest.'

Huldbrand shuddered as he remembered the strange beings who had startled him as he rode through the wood. He glanced distrustfully toward the window. Were the grim figures there, peering at him through the window-pane? No, he could see nothing save the dim night light, which now closed them in.

The knight drew himself up, ashamed of his foolish fears, and turning toward the maiden, he was beginning to tell her of the wonders which had befallen him, when the fisherman hurriedly interrupted.

'Nay, now, Sir Knight,' he cried, 'tell not your tale until the hours of dark have passed.'

At her foster-father's words Undine sprang angrily from the footstool and stood before him. Her eyes flashed and grew larger, colder.

'You say to the stranger not to tell his tale, father,' she cried, 'you say to him not to answer me. But he shall speak, he shall, he shall!' And in her anger she stamped her little feet.

The knight wellnigh smiled as he watched the maiden's wrath, but the old man was grieved that the stranger should see the wayward behaviour of his foster-child, and he reproved her for her anger. The old woman also muttered her displeasure.

Then Undine slipped quickly toward the door of the little cottage. She did not choose to listen to these rebukes.

'I will not stay with you, for you do nothing but scold me, and you will not do anything that I wish,' she cried, and before they could reach her she had opened the door, and was away and out, out into the dark night.

CHAPTER II

UNDINE IS LOST

Huldbrand and the fisherman sprang after the maiden, but when they reached the door of the cottage and looked out into the night she was nowhere to be seen, nor could they catch the sound of her tiny feet to guide them whither she had fled.

The knight looked in astonishment at his host. Was the beautiful maiden only another of the wonderful beings who had bewildered him in the forest? Was she some lovely elf or sprite who had come but to vex them with her pranks?

But as he looked at the old man standing by his side, and saw the tears streaming from his eyes, he knew it was for no spirit of the wood that he thus grieved.

'Alas,' sighed the fisherman, 'this is not the first time that the maiden has treated us thus. It may be she will not return the livelong night, and until she returns it is not possible that we should close our eyes. For what terror may not seize upon her as she wanders hither and thither in the darkness.'

'We must follow her, father, follow her without delay!' cried the young knight.

'Nay,' answered the fisherman, 'my limbs are stiff. Though I knew whither she had fled, I could never follow with speed enough to reach her. Ever she would vanish as I drew near, for she is fleet, fleet as an arrow from the bow.'

'If we may not follow her, at least let us call and entreat her to return,' said the young knight, and without waiting for an answer he called, 'Undine! Undine!'

But the old man shook his head. 'It is useless to call,' he said, 'the little one will not heed your voice.' Yet still the knight's cry rang out into the night, 'Undine, dear Undine, I pray you return!'

No answer came back from the darkness, and at length Huldbrand returned with the fisherman to the cottage.

The old woman, who seemed little troubled by Undine's flight, had gone to bed and the fire was wellnigh out. But the fisherman, drawing the ashes together, placed wood on the top of them, and soon the fire blazed brightly.

Then in the light of the flames they sat and talked, yet they thought only of Undine. The window rattled. They raised their heads to listen. The rain fell in heavy drops, pitter, patter. They thought it was the tread of tiny feet.

'It is she, it is Undine!' they would cry, yet still the maiden did not come. Then they shook their heads sadly, but as they went on talking they listened still.

'It was fifteen years ago, on such a night of wind and rain, that she came,' murmured the old man. 'Our home was sad and desolate, for we had lost our own little child.'

'Ah,' said the knight, 'tell me how the beautiful maiden came to your little cottage.'

Now this is the story the fisherman told to the knight.

'It is fifteen years ago,' began the old man, 'since I went through the forest, hoping to sell my fish in the city beyond. I was alone, for my wife was at home watching our little babe. Our little babe was dear to us and very fair.

'In the evening, having sold all my fish, I went home through the haunted forest, nor did I fear its gloom, for the Lord was at my right hand.

'But no sooner had I left the wood than I saw my wife running toward me, while tears streamed from her eyes. She had dressed herself, I noticed, in black garments, and this she was not used to do. I felt sure that trouble had befallen us.

'"Where is our child, our little one?" I cried, though even as I spoke my voice was choked with sobs.

'"Our child is with God, the great Father," answered my wife.

'Then in the midst of her tears the poor mother told her sad tale.

'"I took our child down to the edge of the lake, and there we played together, so happy, so merry. Suddenly the little one bent forward as though she saw something beautiful in the water. Then she smiled, and stretched out her tiny hands, and even as she did so, she slipped from my arms into the lake, and I saw her no more."

'That evening,' said the fisherman, 'my wife and I sat by our hearth in silence, we were too sad for words. Suddenly the door of our cottage flew open, and there before us,[1] on the threshold, stood a little maiden, three or four years of age. Her eyes were blue and her hair was gold and she was clothed in beautiful garments.

'We gazed in wonder at the tiny vision. Who was she? From whence had she come? Was she only a magic child come to mock us in our loneliness, or was she a real, a living child?

'Then as we looked we saw that water trickled from her golden hair and that little streams were gathering at her tiny feet, as the water dripped and dripped from her beautiful clothing.

'"She must have fallen into the lake," I said to my wife, "and in some strange way have wandered into our cottage. We have lost our own dear child, let us now do all we can to help this little one." Thus it came to pass that the little stranger slept in the cot in which until now our own babe had lain.

'When morning dawned my wife fed our tiny guest with bread and milk, and the little one looked upon us, and her blue eyes danced merrily, but never a word did she say.

---

[1] See frontispiece.

'We asked her where her father and mother dwelt and how she had come to our cottage. But her only answer was some childish talk of crystal palaces and shining pearls. Even now indeed she speaks of things so marvellous that we know not what to think.

'After some days we asked her once again from whence she came. She told us that she had been on the sea with her mother, and had fallen from her arms into the water, nor had she known more until she awoke under the trees, close to our cottage, so well pleased with the fair shore that she felt no fear.

'Then we said, "Let us keep the little stranger, and care for her as we would have cared for our own lost child." We sent for a priest, who baptized her, giving her the name by which she called herself, though indeed it seemed no name for a Christian child.

'"Undine," said the priest as he performed the holy rite, while she, the little one, stood before him gentle and sweet. No sooner, however, was the service ended than she grew wild, wilful as was her way. For it is true that my wife has had much trouble with the maiden—'

At that moment the knight interrupted the fisherman.

'Listen,' he cried, 'how the stream roars as it dashes past the window!'

Together they sprang to the door. The moon had risen, and the knight and the fisherman saw that the stream which ran from the wood had burst its banks. It was now rushing wildly along, carrying with it stones and roots of trees. As they looked, the clouds grew dark and crept across the face of the moon, the wind rose and lashed the water of the lake into great waves.

'Undine! Undine!' cried the two men together, but no answer reached them save the shrieking of the wind among the trees of the forest.

Then, careless of the storm, the fisherman and the knight rushed from the cottage in search of the maiden.

CHAPTER III

UNDINE IS FOUND

As Huldbrand rushed out into the night, followed by the fisherman, the storm seemed to rage yet more fiercely. The old man was soon left far behind in the search for the lost maiden.

The knight, battling bravely with the storm, hastened hither and thither, but all his efforts were vain. Undine was nowhere to be found.

And now, as the rain dashed down upon him and the wind hustled him, Huldbrand grew bewildered. The storm seemed to have changed the peaceful meadows into a weary wilderness, and even the maiden herself seemed to flit before him as a phantom spirit of the wind.

Could it all have been but a dream? Had the cottage, the fisherman and his wife been as unreal as the figures that had followed him in the haunted forest? No, that he would not believe, for even yet in the distance he could hear the faint echo of the fisherman's voice as he called out pitifully, 'Undine! Undine!' Now in his search the knight had reached the edge of the stream. The stream, as you know, had already overflowed its bank, and as the moon suddenly shone through the dark clouds, Huldbrand saw that the water was rushing back toward the forest. In this way the little bit of meadow-land on which the fisherman's cottage stood was turned into an island.

A terrible thought struck the knight. Had Undine strayed into the fearful forest she could not now return to the cottage, save across the raging stream, nay, she might even now be surrounded by the spirits of the wood. She would be among them alone, helpless.

At once Huldbrand made up his mind to cross the torrent. He plunged into the water, and even as he did so he seemed to see on the other shore the figure of a tall white man, who nodded his head and mocked him as he struggled on. Huldbrand knew the tall white figure only too well. It was the one that had followed him as he journeyed through the forest.

Now; in his haste to find Undine, the knight was leaping from stone to stone, sometimes slipping into the water, then with a struggle placing his feet once again upon the stones. These, tossed by the rushing stream, gave no firm foothold to the knight, and he was forced to seize the branch of a fir-tree to help him across the dangerous passage.

While he was still in the midst of the current, he heard a sweet voice crying,

'Trust not the stream, trust it not, for it is full of craft!'

The knight knew the voice. It was that of the maiden for whom he sought. Yet though he peered eagerly through the gloom he could see no trace of her.

'See! you can find me now, Sir Knight, for the moon is shining clear,' cried the voice he longed to hear, and looking around him Huldbrand saw where Undine had found a shelter. It was on a little island, beneath the branches of a great tree, that the maiden sat. There was no terror of the storm in her eyes. She was even smiling happily as she nestled amid the sweet scented grass, safe from the fury of the storm.

A few quick strides and the knight had crossed the stream and stood by the side of the maiden. She bade him sit down on the grass, and then, whispering low, she said, 'You shall tell me your story here, Sir Knight, on this quiet island here, where no cross old people will disturb us, and where we are sheltered from the storm that rages beyond.'

AMID THE SWEET-SCENTED GRASS, SAFE FROM THE FURY OF THE STORM

Then Huldbrand forgot all about the old man who was still seeking for his child, forgot too all about the old woman who was alone in the little cottage by the lake, and he sat down to tell his tale as the maiden wished.

Meanwhile the fisherman had reached the brink of the stream, and great was his surprise to see the knight seated by the side of his lost child.

'You have found her, you have found my little one!' he cried reproachfully. 'Why did you not hasten to tell me she was found, Sir Knight?'

Then Huldbrand was ashamed, though, as he told the old man, it was but a little while since his search had ceased.

'Bring her without more delay to the mainland!' shouted the fisherman, when he had listened to the sorry excuse which was all the knight could offer.

But Undine had no wish to go home. She would rather stay with the knight in the forest than go back to the cottage, for there, so she said, no one would do as she wished.

Then, flinging her arms around the knight, she clung to him and begged him to stay with her in the forest.

The old fisherman wept as he heard her words, yet Undine did not seem to notice his tears. But the knight could not help seeing the old man's grief, and he was troubled.

'Undine,' he cried, 'the tears of your foster-father have touched my heart. We will return to him.'

The blue eyes of the maiden opened wide with surprise, yet she answered gently, 'Sir Knight, if this is indeed your will, we shall return to the mainland. There you must make the old man promise to listen in silence to all that you saw as you journeyed through the forest.'

'Only come, and you shall do all that you wish!' cried the fisherman, and he stretched out his arms and nodded his head, to show to the maiden how glad he was that she should do as she wished. But the knight shuddered as his eyes fell upon the fisherman. The nodding head, the white hair reminded him once again of the tall white man of the forest.

Shaking off his fears he lifted Undine in his arms and bore her across the stream. Already the storm was wellnigh over and the waters flowed more quietly. It now seemed to the knight only a few steps from the grassy plot where he had found the maiden to the green meadows among which the cottage stood.

'Now will I hear the brave knight's story,' cried the maiden, and the old people smiled and said they too would hear the tale.

And the sun rose slowly over the lake and the birds sang merrily on the wet and leafy trees, as the knight began his tale.

CHAPTER IV

THE KNIGHT'S STORY

'It must be about eight days ago now,' said the knight, 'since I left my castle of Ringstetten, and journeyed toward the city which lies beyond the haunted forest.

'The city was gay with lords and ladies who had come thither for the tournament which was then being held.

'I at once entered the lists, for my steed was strong and I myself was eager for the fray. Once, as I rested from the combat, my eyes fell upon a lady who was wondrous fair. She was looking down from a gallery upon the tournament.

'Bertalda was the name of the beautiful maiden, and she was the foster-child of a great duke. I knew that, as I again seized my lance, the lady's eyes followed me into the lists, and I fought even more bravely than before.

'In the evening a great festival was held, and here I met Bertalda, and danced with her; indeed, evening after evening we were together until the tournament drew to a close.'

As Huldbrand spoke these words he felt a sharp pain in his left hand. It was hanging by his side, and as he looked down to see what had caused the pain, he found that Undine had fastened in it her little pearly teeth.

The knight could see that the maiden's face was no longer smiling. She looked up at him, and there was sorrow in her large blue eyes as she whispered, 'Sir Knight, it is your own fault that I hurt you. I would not have you praise the lady Bertalda.' Then quickly, as though ashamed of her words, she hid her face in her hands.

As the knight went on with his story, his face was grave.

'It is true,' he said, 'that Bertalda was a lovely maiden, yet as I knew her better I found her ways were cold and proud. She pleased me less as the days passed by, though, as she looked upon me with favour, I begged that as a token of it she would give me a glove.

"You shall have it," answered she, "if you will go alone through the forest which men say is haunted, and bring me tidings of all that happens to you."

'I cared little for her glove, but I would not tarry to be asked a second time to go through the forest, lest the maiden should doubt my courage.'

'I thought Bertalda had loved you,' cried Undine, 'yet then had she not driven you from her into the haunted forest.'

The knight smiled at the maiden's words and went on with his tale.

'It was but yesterday morning that I set forth on my adventure. The sun shone bright, so bright that it was not easy to believe that evil was lurking in the shadows beneath the rustling leaves. "I shall soon return," I said to myself, as I plunged into the green shade.

'But amid the maze of trees it was not long ere I lost sight of the path by which I had entered the wood.

'"It may be that I shall lose myself in this mighty forest," I thought, "but no other danger threatens me."

'I gazed up toward the sun, which had risen higher now than when first I entered the wood, and as I gazed I saw a black thing among the branches of a leafy oak.

'Was it a bear, I wondered, and my hand felt for the sword that hung by my side.

'But it was no bear, for ere long I heard a voice mocking me with rough and cruel words. "Aha, Sir Wiseacre," said the voice, "I am breaking twigs off these tall trees, so that at midnight I may light a fire in which to roast you." Then, before I could answer, the black thing grinned at me and rustled the branches, until my steed grew restless and at length galloped away.'

Undine looked at the knight, her blue eyes sparkling as she cried, 'But indeed the wicked creature did not dare to roast you, Sir Knight!'

'In its terror,' continued Huldbrand, 'my horse dashed itself against the trees, reared and again rushed madly forward. Onward we flew, until at length I saw before me a dark abyss. Yet still I found it impossible to pull up my frightened steed.

'Then all at once a tall white man stood still directly in front of my maddened horse, which swerved aside as soon as it saw the tall man, and in that moment I was once more master of my steed. I saw also that my deliverer was not a tall white man, as I had imagined, but a brook, which shone silver in the sunlight.'

'Dear brook, I will be grateful to you for evermore,' cried Undine, clapping her hands as she spoke, in childish glee. But the fisherman shook his head and was silent.

'And now,' said the knight, 'I was anxious to hasten as quickly as possible through the forest, for it seemed to me that not only might I find it difficult to regain the pathway I had lost, but that strange beings might again startle both me and my noble steed.

'I turned my horse away from the dark chasm which lay before us, but even as I did so I found at my side a strange little man. He was uglier than any one I had ever seen. His nose was wellnigh as large as all the rest of his body, and his mouth was so big that it stretched from one ear to the other.

'This ugly creature, as soon as he saw that I had noticed him, grinned at me, until his mouth looked even larger than before. He scraped his feet along the ground and bowed mockingly to me a thousand times.

'My horse was trembling at the sight of the strange figure, so I resolved to ride on in search of further adventure, or if I found none, to ride back to the city which I had left in the morning.

'But the ugly little man did not mean to let me escape. Quick as lightning he sprang round and stood again in front of my horse.

'"Get out of the way," I now cried in anger, "lest my steed tramples you under its feet."

'This did not seem to frighten the strange creature. He laughed in my face, and then said in a gruff voice, "You must give me gold, for it was I who turned your horse aside from yonder dark abyss."

'"Nay, what you say is not true," I answered him, "for it was the silver brook that saved me and my horse from being dashed to pieces. Nevertheless, take thy gold and begone."

'As I spoke I flung a coin into the strange-shaped cap which he was holding before me, then putting spurs to my horse I rode quickly forward.

'I heard the ugly little man give a loud scream, then to my surprise there he was, running by my side, grinning and making horrible grimaces.

'My horse was galloping, and I thought I would soon get away from the little man. But it seemed impossible to go faster than he, for he took a spring, a jump, and there he was still by my side. He held up the piece of gold I had thrown to him, and in a hollow voice he cried, "It is a false coin, a false coin!"

'At length I could bear his horrible shrieks no longer. I pulled up my steed, and holding out two coins I called to him, "Take the gold, but follow me no farther!"

'Then the little ugly man began to scrape his feet and bow his head, but it was plain that he was not yet satisfied.

'"I do not wish your gold," he grumbled. "I have gold enough and to spare, as you shall soon see."

'As he spoke a strange thing happened. The beautiful green ground seemed to change into clear green glass. I looked through the glass and saw in a great cavern a group of little goblins.

'They were playing at ball, these little goblins, and I noticed that all their toys were made of silver or gold. Merry little creatures they were, running swiftly hither and thither after the ball, nor was it easy to see whether they were standing on their heads or on their heels, or whether they were running on their hands or on their feet. No sooner was their game ended than they pelted each other with their playthings, then in a mad frolic lifted handfuls of gold dust and flung it each in the other's eyes.

'All this time the ugly little man was standing half on the ground and half within the great cavern where the tiny goblins played their games. Now I heard him call to the mischievous imps to give him handfuls of gold.

'I SAW IN A GREAT CAVERN A GROUP OF LITTLE GOBLINS'

'This they did, and then he, laughing in my face, showed the gold to me ere he flung it back again into the cavern.

'Then the ugly little man called to the tiny goblins to stop their pranks and look at the coins I had given to him. When they caught sight of them they held their little sides, shaking with laughter; then all at once they turned and hissed at me.

'In spite of myself terror crept over me. Again I plunged my spurs into my horse's sides, and it dashed madly off into the midst of the forest.

'When at length the flight ended, the evening lay cool and quiet around me. A white footpath seemed to point out the way which led back to the city. But each time I tried to approach it a face peered at me from between the trees. I turned to escape from this new phantom, but in vain, for whichever way I turned there was the face still staring at me.

'I grew angry and urged my horse in the direction of the shadowy face, only however to find myself drenched by a stream of white foam.

'Thus I was driven away from the white footpath, and only one way, rough and tangled, was left open to me. As soon as I began to follow it, the face, though it kept close behind, did me no further harm.

'Yet again and again I turned, hoping to find that the face had disappeared. Instead I found it closer than before, and now I could see that it belonged to a tall white man. It was true that at times the long white figure seemed to be but a wandering stream, but of this I was never sure.

I was weary now and my horse was exhausted. It seemed useless to try any longer to force my way past the white face, so I went on riding quietly along the one path left open to me. The head of the tall man then began to nod, as though to say that at length I was doing as he wished.

'By this path I reached the end of the wood, and as the meadows and the lake came into sight the white man vanished, and I found myself standing near to your little cottage.'

As the knight had now finished the story of his adventure, the fisherman began to talk to his guest of how he might return in safety to the city and to the followers who there awaited him.

Huldbrand, listening to the old man, yet caught the soft ripple of Undine's laughter.

'Why do you laugh, Undine?' asked the knight. 'Are you so pleased to hear your foster-father talk of my return to the city?'

'I laugh for joy that you cannot leave us,' said the maiden. 'You have but to look to see that you must stay.'

Huldbrand and the fisherman rose and saw that what the maiden had said was indeed true. It would not be possible for the knight to leave the little island until the stream had once more returned to its usual course.

As they entered the cottage, Huldbrand whispered to the maiden, 'Undine, tell me that you are glad that I cannot yet return to the crowded city.'

But the maiden's face was no longer glad, nor would she answer the knight's question. She had remembered Bertalda.

When the stream had grown quiet the knight would go back to the lady for whose sake he had undergone such strange perils. And of that time the wilful maiden did not wish to think.

CHAPTER V

THE KNIGHT STAYS AT THE COTTAGE

Day after day the forest stream rushed wildly on. The bed along which it thus hastened grew wider and wider, separating the island with the fisherman's cottage yet farther from the mainland.

The knight was well pleased to linger where he was. Never had he found the days pass by so swiftly.

He discovered an old crossbow in a corner of the cottage. When he had mended it he would wander forth in search of birds, and if he succeeded in bringing some down with his arrows, he would carry them back to fill the larder of the little cottage.

And Undine, for she was pitiful, would not fail to upbraid the knight for taking the life of the little birds, so glad, so free. Seeing them lying there, quiet and still, she would weep.

Yet, did Huldbrand return without his prey, so wilful was the maiden that she would blame him, and complain that she could now have nought to eat save fish or crabs.

But the knight loved Undine's wayward words. And well he knew that after she had shown her anger most, she would in but a little while be again kind and gentle as before.

On the quiet island Huldbrand heard no call to knightly deeds. His sword hung unused on the cottage wall, his steed fed undisturbed among the sweet-scented meadows.

'The maiden is the daughter of a great prince, thought the knight. 'It is not possible that she should remain in this humble cottage all her life. She shall be my bride, and in days to come she shall dwell in my castle of Ringstetten on the banks of the Danube.'

Meanwhile, naught disturbed the dwellers in the little cottage, save now and again when her foster-mother would chide Undine in the presence of the knight.

Now, though this displeased Huldbrand, he could not blame the old woman, for it was ever true that the maiden deserved reproof more often than she received it.

At length wine and food began to grow scarce in the little cottage. In the evening, when the wind howled around their home, the fisherman and the knight had been used to cheer themselves with a flask of wine. But now that the fisherman was not able to reach the city, his supply of wine had come to an end. Without it the old man and the knight grew silent and dull.

Undine teased them, laughed at them, but they did not join in her merriment.

Then one evening the maiden left the cottage, to escape, so she said, from the gloomy faces in the little kitchen. It was a stormy night, and as it grew dark the wind began to blow, the waters to rise. Huldbrand and the fisherman thought of the terrible night on which they had sought so long in vain for the wilful maiden. They even began to fear that they had lost her again, and together they rushed to the door. But to their great delight Undine was standing there, laughing and clapping her little hands.

'Come with me,' she cried when she saw them, 'come with me and I will show you a cask which the stream has thrown ashore. If it is not a wine cask you may punish me as you will.'

The men went with her, and there in a little creek they found the cask and began to roll it toward the cottage.

But though they rolled it rapidly the storm crept quickly up. So black were the clouds, so threatening, that it seemed each moment that the rain would burst forth upon them.

Undine helped the men to roll the cask, and as the sky grew yet more threatening she looked up at the dark clouds and said in a warning voice, 'Beware, beware that you wet us not.'

'It is wrong of you thus to try to rebuke the storm,' said her foster-father, but at his words the maiden only laughed low to herself in the darkness.

It would seem, however, that Undine's warning had been of use, for it was not until the cask was rolled in at the cottage door that the storm broke.

By the bright glow of the fire they opened the cask and found that it did indeed hold wine. They tasted it and found it very good, and soon they were once more as gay as the maiden could wish.

Then suddenly the fisherman grew grave, grieving for him who had lost the cask.

'Nay, grieve not,' said the knight, 'I will seek for the owner and repay him for his loss when I come again to my castle at Ringstetten.'

The fisherman smiled and was content.

Undine, however, was angry with the knight. 'It is foolish,' said she, 'to talk of seeking for the owner of the cask. Were you lost in the search I should weep. Would you not rather stay by my side?'

'Yes, and that do you right well know,' answered the knight.

'Then,' said the maiden, 'why should you speak of helping other people. It is but foolish talk.'

The foster-mother sighed as she listened to Undine's careless words, while the fisherman forgot his usual quiet and scolded her sharply.

'Your words are wild, and are such as no Christian maiden should utter,' he said. 'May God forgive both you and those who have allowed you thus to speak.'

'It is indeed true,' said Undine, 'that as I think I speak. Why, therefore, should you scold me for my words.'

'Say no more,' said the fisherman, for he was very angry.

Then the maiden, who, for all her wilfulness, was timid as a bird, drew close to the knight and whispered, 'Are you also angry with me, Sir Knight.'

Huldbrand could find no words with which to comfort the maiden, whom he had learned to love. He could only hold her hand and stroke her golden hair, but with this Undine was well content.

CHAPTER VI

THE WEDDING

Now it was on this same night on which the cask was found that, as the storm still raged, a knock was heard at the cottage door. It startled all within, for who was there could have crossed the stream that now separated them from the mainland? It could surely be no mortal who stood without.

As the inhabitants of the little cottage sat silent, thinking these thoughts, the knock was heard again. It was followed by a low groan. Then the knight rose and took his sword from the wall where it had hung for many days. But the fisherman, watching him, shook his head as he muttered, 'A sword will be of but little use to-night.'

Undine meanwhile had gone toward the door. She did not open it, but she called out in a loud voice, 'Remember, whoever you be, spirit of earth or fire, that if harm befall us my uncle Kühleborn will punish you.'

These strange words made the knight marvel. But a voice answered the maiden, 'I am no wandering spirit, but an old frail man. For the love of God open your door and give me shelter from the storm.'

At these words Undine, holding a lamp high in one hand, flung the door wide open with the other. Before her stood an old priest, who looked upon her with surprise. How came so fair a maiden to be dwelling in so lonely a home? he wondered, and in his bewilderment he stood still outside the shelter and warmth which awaited him.

'Will you not enter, holy Father?' said Undine.

The priest roused himself to thank the beautiful maiden, and then entered the kitchen. Water flowed from his long robe and trickled from his long white beard and snowy locks.

'Come with me, Father,' said the fisherman, and he drew the priest into a little room and made him take off all his wet garments. Then, clad in a suit of dry clothes which belonged to his host, the priest returned to the kitchen.

The old woman pulled forward her own armchair and made the priest sit in it, while Undine brought a little stool and put it beneath the feet of the stranger.

Meanwhile food was placed before the priest. When he had eaten he was refreshed and able to tell his host how he had reached the island.

'It was but yesterday,' he said, 'that I was sailing across the lake, when a sudden storm arose. A wave dashed upon my boat, overturning it and throwing me on to the shore. I lay there stunned for some time. Then, as I slowly recovered my senses, I saw a footpath before me, and following it I reached the shelter of your cottage.'

Then the fisherman said to the priest, 'Unless the stream subsides we shall, I fear, be in need of food. For days I have found it wellnigh impossible to fish in the lake, and even should I be able to do so I could not sell my fish. It would be too hard a task to reach the city beyond the wood until the stream once more runs quietly between its banks.'

To Huldbrand as he listened it mattered not though the stream rushed on for ever. The world beyond the wood was becoming to the knight more and more as a dream. Also the little island on which he was living seemed to him the most beautiful spot on earth, for on it dwelt the maiden he loved so well.

As these thoughts passed through the knight's mind he turned, and saw at once that Undine must have annoyed her foster-mother, for the old woman was casting angry looks upon the maiden. Perhaps the angry looks would be followed by harsh words, as had happened on other days.

Quickly the knight made up his mind. Were Undine but his wife, no one would venture to reprove her. The priest was in the cottage. Why should he not marry the beautiful maiden without delay?

He spoke a few words to Undine, then drawing her gently toward the priest he said, 'Father, you see before you the maiden whom I love, whom, if her foster-parents are willing, I would wed this very day.'

The priest turned to the fisherman and his wife. 'You hear the words of the noble knight,' he said. 'Are you willing that he should wed the maiden?'

It was easy to see that the old people were in no way startled by the priest's words.

'To no braver or more courteous knight could we give our foster-child,' said the fisherman, and his wife smiled and nodded as he spoke.

Then the foster-mother brought two candles, which long years before had been blessed by a holy man, and placed them on the kitchen table, while the knight, unfastening the chain which hung around his neck, began to take off it two golden rings, one for Undine, the other for himself.

'Ah, do not so,' cried the maiden. 'Touch not the golden chain. Believe me, my parents, could they know, would wish us to use the rings they entrusted to my care when I was but a child.'

She ran quickly from the room, and when she came back she held in her hand two radiant rings, one of which she gave to the knight, while the other she kept for herself.

Her foster-parents looked at Undine in surprise, for they had neither seen the rings nor known that their foster-child had any jewels in her possession.

Then the maiden, seeing their astonishment, told how her parents had stitched the rings into the little garments she had worn when first she came to them, a tiny child. 'They bid me also tell no one that they had given me these precious gems until the evening of my wedding-day.'

Meanwhile the priest had clad himself again in his own garments, and lighting the candles, he called to Huldbrand and the maiden to come and kneel before him.

**IN THE LITTLE COTTAGE WERE HEARD THE SOLEMN WORDS
OF THE MARRIAGE SERVICE**

Gladly they obeyed, and then in the little cottage were heard the solemn words of the marriage service, and Undine became the wife of Huldbrand, the knight of Ringstetten.

The maiden had been unusually quiet as she listened to the solemn words of the marriage service, but now a spirit of mischief seemed to seize her. She laughed and danced, she played childish tricks upon her husband, her foster-parents, even upon the priest himself.

Her foster-mother would have rebuked Undine as of old, but the knight silenced her, for Undine was now his wife. Yet he himself was little pleased with her behaviour. When Undine saw a frown upon his brow, it is true that she would grow quieter, and sitting near him, would for a little while smooth his brow with her soft white hand. Soon, however, a new fancy would take hold of her, she would jump up, and her tricks would grow even more vexing than before.

Then the priest spoke, and his voice was grave.

'Lady, you are fair to look on, but I pray you to cease these foolish ways, lest your soul become less beautiful than your face.'

Undine's laughter ceased. After a while she looked at the priest and asked in a timid whisper, 'What is this thing which you call a soul, holy Father?'

Over the little kitchen a hush fell as the holy man answered, 'How can I tell you what this strange thing which we call our soul really is? Yet can I tell you why God gives us this great gift. It is that we may learn to know and love Him. Our bodies will grow old, and we will lay them aside as a garment which we no longer need, while our souls will live and dwell with Him for ever.'

Undine's eyes grew sad, tears streamed down her cheek. 'Ah,' she sobbed, 'I have no soul, no soul. I think it would hurt me to have a soul, yet fain would I have one.'

Then, with one of those quick changes which had at times startled her foster-parents, she dried her tears, and ran quickly to the window. She looked out into the night. It seemed to call her forth to a careless, thoughtless life. Why should she stay when the wind whispered to her and the waters brought her messages from the depths of the sea?

'Ah no, I will have no soul!' cried Undine, turning once more toward the priest. 'I must be free, free as the breezes and the dancing waters.'

'Your love for me will change and grow cold,' said the knight sadly, 'unless you have a human soul. For none can love truly without this precious gift.'

Yet even as he spoke Huldbrand was trying to stifle a fear that had begun to creep into his heart, a fear that the maiden he had wedded was a fairy or a mocking spirit from another world.

But his beautiful wife was smiling softly, for as he had spoken his last words she had learned a secret. And as the knight looked into her blue love-lit eyes he too learned the secret. Through love Undine had won a soul, which is indeed the gift of God to every mortal.

CHAPTER VII

UNDINE'S STORY

Undine lost her wilful ways on her wedding-day.

Her foster-parents watched her, bewildered, so gentle was she, so thoughtful. She, who had but seldom flung her arms around them, embraced them now, and thanked them with tears in her eyes for all their care. Nor would she let them go, until she saw that the old woman wished to prepare breakfast.

Then she herself flew to the hearth, and making her foster-mother rest, she swept and dusted, and prepared the meal. It was strange that she had never thought of doing this before.

And those who dwelt with her, as they watched her grow so gracious, so gentle, learned to love her even more than in the days when she had been wild and wilful.

One evening Undine, with Huldbrand by her side, wandered along the bank of the forest stream.

The knight marvelled that the waters had suddenly grown peaceful, and that now again they were gliding quietly along their usual course.

'To-morrow,' said his fair wife sorrowfully, 'to-morrow you can ride forth where you will.'

'But,' said Huldbrand, 'you know well that if I go I will not leave you behind.'

'I do not think you will leave me, Huldbrand. Yet carry me across to yonder little island, for there I will tell to you the story of the maiden you have made your wife. It may be that when you have heard it, you will ride away alone into the wide world.'

Then silently the knight carried her, as she wished, across the stream to the tiny island, and laid her down on the green grass. It was on this very spot that he had found her on the night of the terrible storm.

'Sit there, where I can look into your eyes as I tell my tale,' said his wife, 'for as I look I shall be able to see what you are thinking, nor will there be any need for you to tell me.'

'In the world,' said Undine, 'there are many beings whom mortals seldom see, for should these beings hear a mortal drawing near, they quickly hide themselves. These beings of whom I tell you are spirits that dwell in fire, earth, air and water.

'Those who dwell in the flames are called salamanders, nor do these spirits wish for any other home, as they play merrily and fearlessly among the sparkling fires.

'Deep under the earth live the gnomes, rough and fearsome spirits they, full of malice too, should any mortal cross their path.

'In lofty forests dwell more fair and joyous spirits, guarding each some well-loved spot from a mortal's heavy tread.

'And better known and better loved than these of whom I have told you are the spirits who haunt the waters. These have their home in sea or lake, in river or in little brook.

'Deep down under the blue waters, hidden from mortal eyes, are the palaces of the water spirits. Their walls are built of crystal and are hung with coral, their floors are paved with shining pearls.

'Deep down under the blue waters are yellow sands. There the merry little water-spirits play their games and gambol all the glad long days, until they leave their childhood far behind.

'Pure and fair, more fair even than the race of mortals are the spirits of the water. Fishermen have chanced to see these water-nymphs or mermaidens, and they have spoken of their wondrous beauty. Mortals too have named these strange women Undines. Look upon me, Huldbrand, look long and well, for I, your wife, am an Undine!'

The knight gazed sadly upon his beautiful wife. He wished to believe that she was but weaving fairy tales with which to charm him through the quiet eventide, yet as he gazed upon her he shuddered lest the tale she told was true.

Undine saw that he shuddered, and tears sprang into her blue eyes as she went on with her story.

'When I was a child I lived in the depths of the sea. My father's crystal palace was my home, for he, my father, is the Lord of the Ocean. Kühleborn is my uncle. He used to watch me with his big eyes until I grew afraid, and even now, although I live above the waters, he comes to me and ofttimes he frightens me as though I were again a little child.

'Brothers and cousins, too, were mine and played with me on the yellow sands beneath the blue sea.

'Merry were our lives and free, for the sorrows of mortals came not near to us. We had no soul, the gift God gives to every mortal, and without a soul no pain could enter into our lives.

'Yet my father, the King of the Ocean, longed that I, his only daughter, should gain the great gift which is given to every mortal. And this he wished, though well he knew that to mortals was given, with the gift of a soul, the power to suffer.

'An Undine can gain a soul in one way alone. She must love and be loved by one of mortal birth.

'You, Huldbrand, you have given me my soul, and should you now despise me or drive me from you, I should suffer even as one of your own race.

'Yet if you care not to have an Undine for your wife, leave me, and I will plunge into the waters. Then Kühleborn, my uncle, who brought me a merry happy child to the fisherman, will come and carry me back to my ocean home. There will I live, loving, sorrowing, for into the depths of the blue sea will I carry my new-won soul.'

Then Huldbrand forgot everything save the great love he bore his fair wife Undine. He took her in his arms and carried her across the little stream, whispering to her that she should never leave him.

Together they went back to the cottage, and to the water-maiden the little dwelling gleamed more bright than the crystal palace of the Ocean King.

CHAPTER VIII

HULDBRAND AND UNDINE LEAVE THE COTTAGE

The following day Undine was up and out early in the morning, to see if the forest stream was still flowing quietly within its banks. Now the forest stream was the one haunted by her uncle Kühleborn, and often he would use the waters for his own purposes. Sometimes Kühleborn's purposes were kind, sometimes they were unkind.

Undine was, in the cottage again, preparing the morning meal, when Huldbrand entered the kitchen. She greeted him brightly.

'My uncle Kühleborn has made the waters calm,' she cried. 'The stream is gliding peaceful as of old through the forest. Neither in air nor water are there spirits to molest us. Should you wish it, you can journey homeward to-day.'

Huldbrand did not like to hear Undine speak of her strange kinsfolk, yet so gentle was she, so full of grace, that he soon forgot his vexation.

Together the knight and his wife went to the door of the cottage, and looked out at the meadows and the lake lying in the morning sunshine.

'Why should we leave this quiet spot to-day?' said Huldbrand, for well he loved the island where he had found his beautiful bride. 'In the great world we will spend no gladder days than in this simple meadow-land. Let us, then, yet linger here for a few days.'

'It shall be as you wish,' answered Undine. 'Yet will my foster-parents grieve the more when I leave them, should they learn that I have now a soul. To-day they only marvel that I am kind and thoughtful, thinking that to-morrow I will once again be wild and careless as of old. But should I dwell here much longer they will know that never in the days to come will I be thoughtless as in former days. For I cannot hide my new gift. They will hear it in my voice, they will feel it in my touch, they will see it in my eyes. And having known that now, at length, I could love them well, they would grieve to lose me.'

'We will leave to-day, this very hour,' said the knight, so pleased was he with Undine's new care for her kind old foster-parents.

The priest who had found shelter in the cottage was also ready to return to his monastery. He would journey with the knight and his lady until they were safe from the perils of the haunted wood.

Accordingly they sought the fisherman and his wife, and told them that now they must leave the shelter of their cottage and journey toward the city that lay beyond the forest.

The farewells were said and Huldbrand lifted his beautiful wife and seated her on his horse. He himself would walk by her side.

The three travellers soon reached the leafy shades of the forest.

On one side of the lady walked the priest, clad in a long white robe, while, guarding her on the other side, was, as I told you, the knight. His armour was burnished and his sword was once more girt by his side.

As Huldbrand and Undine talked joyfully together, a stranger joined the priest, yet they in their joy did not notice this.

The stranger wore a garment such as a monk might wear. The hood was drawn forward and wellnigh hid his face, while the whole robe hung loosely around him, in great folds, so that at each step he must gather it up and throw it over his arm.

**THE THREE TRAVELLERS SOON REACHED THE LEAFY SHADES
OF THE FOREST**

'I have lived in the forest for many years,' said the stranger to the priest, 'and I love it for its great beauty. As I flit in and out among the dark shadows of the trees, I play with the stray sunbeams as they cast their glances here and there on my white robe.'

'Tell me your name, for I would fain know who you are,' said the priest to his companion.

'Nay, tell me first who are you who ask?' said the stranger.

'Father Heilman is my name,' answered the priest, 'and I am journeying back to my monastery, after an absence of many days.'

'Now I,' said the stranger, 'am named Lord Kühleborn, though sometimes I am called Kühleborn the Free, for indeed I am free as the wild birds of the air to go hither and thither as I will. Meanwhile, Sir Priest, I bid you farewell, for I would speak to yonder lady.'

Even as he spoke, Kühleborn left the priest and came close up to Undine. He bent forward as though he would whisper in her ear. But Undine drew herself quickly away, crying as she saw who was by her side, 'I no longer wish to have aught to do with you!'

But her uncle only laughed at her words.

'You are my niece,' he said, 'and I am here to guide you through the forest. The goblins in the cavern beneath the earth might come forth to do you harm were I not here to keep them quiet. The priest, who is named Father Heilman, speaks to me more kindly than do you. Know you not that it was I who brought him in safety to the little island to be ready for your wedding-day?'

Undine and the knight turned to the priest, but he was walking as one in deep thought, and had, it was easy to see, heard nothing that the stranger had said.

Then Undine turned again to her uncle. 'See yonder,' she cried, 'I can see already the end of the wood. We need your help no longer. I pray you vanish and do not disturb us further.'

When Kühleborn saw that Undine really wished him to leave her, he was angry. He made faces and shook his fist at his niece, until at length she screamed, 'Huldbrand, Huldbrand, save me, I entreat you!'

The knight at once drew his sword and would have struck at the rude stranger. But as he thrust in the direction of Kühleborn he felt a waterfall come rushing down from a rock above him. He drew his wife back, that she might not be drenched, but as he did so a white spray was flung after them which wet them both to the skin. At that moment they heard, as they thought, a low mocking laugh.

'It is strange,' said the priest, 'that the ripple of the stream should sound almost as the voice of a man.'

To Huldbrand the stream still seemed to be speaking, and these were the words he thought he heard. 'You were foolish, Sir Knight, to draw your sword, yet will I not be angry with you, nor will I quarrel with you so long as you guard well your beautiful wife. Yet be not again thus hasty, Sir Knight.'

As the voice faded away into silence the travellers reached the end of the wood. Before them was the city, glowing red in the rays of the setting sun.

CHAPTER IX

THE KNIGHT RETURNS TO THE CITY

Now all this time the lady Bertalda had been very unhappy because of the knight's long absence. Indeed, she had no sooner sent Huldbrand forth into the haunted forest than she began to wish that she had kept him by her side. As day after day passed and he did not return, she grew fearful lest he had lost his way and perished in the mazes of the wood. When a little later she heard of the floods that had made the country around impassable, she wellnigh lost all hope of his return.

In spite of this, however, she begged the knights who had taken part in the tournament to go in search of Huldbrand, but this they were unwilling to do.

As for the knight's own servants, they would not leave the city without their master, yet neither would they follow him into the dreaded forest. They lingered on at an inn of the city, lamenting his absence, but doing nought to bring him back.

It was now, when there seemed but little hope of his return, that Huldbrand, to the surprise of every one, appeared in the city, bringing with him a wife of wondrous beauty, as well as Father Heilman, the priest who had married them.

Huldbrand's servants rejoiced to see their young master alive and well. And the town folk, who had heard of his disappearance, were glad that the light-hearted knight, who had always treated them with courtesy, had suffered no harm in his adventure.

But the lady Bertalda, though she was glad that the knight had returned, was sad when she saw that he had not come back alone. She herself had loved him, and had hoped that, if ever he should return, he would claim her as his bride.

Yet though Bertalda was sad, she was a wise maiden, and she received Undine kindly, thinking that she was a princess whom Huldbrand had rescued from a wicked wizard. For the true story of the beautiful Undine was known to none, save to the knight alone.

As for Undine, she no sooner saw Bertalda than she loved her, and begged her to stay in the city until she and her husband left it. Nay, more, she even asked the maiden to promise to go with them when they set out for the castle of Ringstetten, which stood on the banks of the river Danube, and Bertalda was well pleased with this request.

One evening they three together walked up and down in the public square. In the midst of the square stood a beautiful fountain, and here they lingered to watch the water as it tumbled and tossed. So violently did it do this that it seemed as though the fountain must break, and the water, bursting its bonds, must flow away far and free.

At that moment a tall man came towards them from the market-place, and, bowing to the knight and Bertalda, he drew the young wife aside that he might speak to her alone.

Huldbrand looked at the stranger, and as he looked he felt sure that he had seen him before. He grew a little angry, this hasty knight, as he watched his wife and the stranger whispering together. He caught a few words too, and they seemed to him to be in a foreign language, and this displeased him yet more.

At this moment, however, Undine left the stranger. As she came toward her husband she was laughing merrily and clapping her hands.

But the stranger, as she left him, shook his head and frowned. Then he walked with great strides toward the fountain, and stepping into it he vanished and was seen no more.

'It is Kühleborn, the spirit of the forest stream—I know him now,' thought Huldbrand to himself.

But Bertalda seemed to see nothing unusual about the stranger. She thought he was the Master of the fountain, and turning to Undine she asked her what the man had said to make her laugh so gaily.

'The day after to-morrow is your birthday, dear Bertalda,' said Undine. 'Wait only until then, and I will tell you the reason of my joy.'

Then, saying farewell to Bertalda, Undine and the knight walked toward their home.

'Was it Kühleborn who spoke to you by the fountain?' asked Huldbrand, and his voice sounded cold, for he did not wish to be reminded of his wife's strange relations.

'It was he,' answered Undine. 'He told me tidings that made me rejoice. I will tell you without delay, should you desire it, what the tidings were. Yet if you will but wait until Bertalda's birthday, you will give me great pleasure, and you yourself will enjoy a great surprise.'

Listening to her gentle words, the knight forgot the ill-humour he had but lately felt, and willingly he agreed to wait until she herself wished to tell him the good news.

And Undine, as she fell asleep that night, was smiling happily. 'Bertalda, dear Bertalda,' she murmured, 'how she will rejoice when I tell her the tidings brought to me by him whom she calls the Master of the fountain.'

CHAPTER X

THE BIRTHDAY FEAST

It had been Undine's wish to give a great banquet in honour of Bertalda's birthday. The knight had ordered that all should be done as she desired.

The feast was now spread, and the guests, of whom there were a great number, had already taken their seats.

At the upper end of the table sat Bertalda, surrounded with flowers and jewels, gifts these which her foster-parents and friends had showered upon her. By her side sat the knight and his fair young wife.

When at length the fruit was placed on the table, the doors of the banqueting-room were flung open. (In Germany, where the knight lived, it was usual to do this that the peasant folk might look in and see how their masters fared.) Wine and cakes were offered to those who on this evening came to show their pleasure in the joy of the knight and his young wife.

Huldbrand and Bertalda, meanwhile, were watching Undine with eager eyes. Had she not a secret to tell them, which, when they knew it, would make them even happier than before?

But Undine only smiled upon them as she caught their eyes, and shook her head slightly as though to say, 'No, it is still too soon, too soon.'

At this moment the guests begged the young mistress of the feast to sing. She seemed pleased with the request, and taking her lute in her hands, she began to play softly, while her clear voice filled the room.

It was a song of sunshine and green grass, of sweet flowers and sparkling waters, and the guests, listening spellbound, forgot all else save the singer and her song.

But hark! the song is changing. Who is the child of whom Undine sings? A child who has been borne by the waves far from the home of her birth. The little one is lying like a flower among the meadow grass (the guests can see her as the singer sings) and reaches out her tiny hands for help.

Ah! now they hear the tramp, tramp of a horse. A noble duke is riding slowly along. He halts, for he sees the little maid. He stoops and lifts her in his arms, and carries her off to his own castle, and surrounds her with splendour and with wealth.

And now tears gather in the eyes of the guests. The song is drawing to a close, and Undine is singing of an unknown shore, where in a little cottage sit a father and mother, desolate and sad, for they have lost their little child, and they know not where to find her.

Among all the guests were none who listened to the song more eagerly than Bertalda's noble foster-parents.

'She has sung the story of Bertalda, the little child we found so long ago,' they said each to the other. 'It was even thus we found her in the meadow, among the flowers.'

And Bertalda herself cried out in haste, 'Undine, Undine, you know my parents, bring them to me, bring them to me, I entreat you!'

Then Undine, with tears that were tears of joy in her eyes, looked at Bertalda, and said softly, 'They are here, your parents are here, dear maiden, and when you see them you will rejoice. Well do I know the tender care they will give to you, for it was even they who were my own foster-parents.'

At a sign from Undine the old fisherman and his wife now stepped forward from the corner in which their foster-child had bidden them wait. It was she, Undine, who had sent for them that they might claim Bertalda, who was, as Kühleborn told her, their child.

The eyes of all the guests were fixed in astonishment on the humble fisherman and his wife. Could these poor working folk be indeed the parents of the maiden who stood before them, so cold, so full of pride?

'Yes, here is your long-lost daughter,' said Undine softly, as the old people stood bewildered before Bertalda. Then they, taking courage from her words, threw their arms around their daughter. And as they embraced her, tears streamed down their old worn faces, while they thanked God for His goodness in giving them back their child.

But Bertalda tore herself from their arms. She, the child of a poor old fisherman and his wife! She could not believe it. She did not wish to believe it. In her pride she had hoped to be known as the daughter of a beautiful princess, or even of a queen. Now in her anger she believed that Undine had brought the fisherman and his wife to the banquet only to crush her pride and to humble her before Huldbrand and his guests.

The angry maiden took no pains to hide her rage. She reproached Undine, Undine who had only wished to give her joy, nor had she any words too bitter to fling at the fisherman and his wife.

And Undine, who had hoped to make her friend and her foster-parents happy, listened sadly, now to Bertalda, now to the old fisherman and his wife.

'Bertalda,' she cried, 'Bertalda, do not be angry. Have you not a soul? Let it teach you not to grieve your parents more.'

But Bertalda only grew more angry, and the poor parents, as they heard her scorn, more sad.

As for the guests, they were talking loudly, some being sorry for the maiden, others for the fisherman and his wife.

Then Undine begged the knight to let her speak to their guests. And he yielding to her wish, she walked to the upper end of the table, and while all eyes were fixed upon her, she spoke.

'My secret, which I thought would cause Bertalda joy, has caused her sorrow. Yet must I tell you that I have spoken the truth. For he who told me was he who, when Bertalda was but a little babe, drew her into the water, and thereafter laid her in the green meadow through which the duke rode toward his castle.'

'Do not listen to her words!' shouted Bertalda in her rage. 'She is a witch, a witch!'

'Nay, I am no witch. Look upon me that you may know,' answered Undine. And as they gazed upon her pure face and into her clear blue eyes, the guests knew that she spoke the truth. Undine was not a witch.

'If she is not a witch, she at least has not told the truth,' cried Bertalda, scorn in her cold voice. 'She has no proof that I am the child of these wretched old people.' Then, turning to her noble foster-parents, she entreated them to take her away at once from the city, where such shame had been brought upon her.

But the duke did not move, while the duchess said in a firm voice, 'We shall not leave this room, nor shall you, proud maiden, until we know the truth.'

Then the fisherman's wife drew near to the noble lady, and curtsying low she said, 'Should this bad maiden be indeed my daughter, as I do think she is, she will have between her shoulders a mark like a violet, and this mark also you will find on the instep of her left foot. Let the maiden come with me that—'

But Bertalda rudely interrupted the old woman's words.

'I will not go with the peasant!' she said.

'But you will come with me into another room,' said the duchess, and Bertalda knew that she would have to go. 'And the old woman shall come with us,' added the noble lady in a kind voice.

As the three went out of the banqueting-room, silence fell upon the guests. Now they would soon know the truth.

Slowly the moments passed. At length the door opened and the duchess returned with Bertalda and the old woman. Bertalda looked pale and frightened.

'It is but just,' said the noble lady, looking round the room, 'it is but just that you should know the truth. It is as our hostess has said. Bertalda is indeed the daughter of the fisherman and his wife.'

The duke and duchess then left the room, followed by their foster-child, the duke bidding Bertalda's true parents come with them also.

In silence the other guests slipped away, to talk in their own homes over all that they had heard and seen, and Undine, left alone with her husband, wept bitterly.

CHAPTER XI
THE JOURNEY TO CASTLE RINGSTETTEN

The knight did all he could to comfort his wife, and although he was sorry to see her tears, he was glad to think that she, who had been so wild and wilful, had now a soul so kind and loving.

'If it is true that Undine has won through love a soul, it is one more pure than mortals know,' he thought to himself.

As he comforted his wife Huldbrand made up his mind to take her away from the city as soon as possible.

In the city the lady Bertalda was well known, and people talked of the strange story of her birth. But among them all none was heard to say an unkind word about Undine, while many there were who blamed Bertalda for her cruel behaviour toward her friend and the poor old fisherman and his wife. But this neither the knight nor his lady knew, nor would it have comforted Undine had she been told.

The morning after the feast a beautiful carriage stood at the door. Huldbrand and his wife were ready to set out on their journey to the castle of Ringstetten.

As the knight and Undine were stepping into the carriage a fisher-girl drew near, and begged them to buy her fish.

'We are leaving the city, we do not need any fish,' said the knight courteously. But at the sound of his voice the girl burst into tears, and Huldbrand saw with surprise that it was Bertalda who had spoken to him.

'Why do you weep so bitterly?' asked Undine, drawing Bertalda into the house, and the maiden, who had no pride left, told her story.

'My foster-parents,' she said between her sobs, 'my foster-parents are so displeased with my cruel behaviour to you and to the old fisherman and his wife, that they no longer wish me to live with them. They have given me a large sum of money and have sent me away into the wide world. The fisherman and his wife, to whom they have also given gifts, have gone back to their cottage by the lake. I was too fearful to wish to be left alone in the world, and fain would I have gone with them to their simple home, but he who is said to be my father—'

AT THE SOUND OF HIS VOICE THE GIRL BURST INTO TEARS

'In truth he is your father,' interrupted Undine, and her voice was grave.

'Even if he be my father,' answered Bertalda, 'yet would he not take me with him to his cottage. Did I care for him or for his wife, he said, I would not fear to journey alone through the haunted forest, until I found my home. Nor would he welcome me should I go to him dressed in aught save the dress of a fisher-girl. Although the thought of the forest makes me tremble, yet will I do as he has said. But first I have come to you, gentle lady,' and as she spoke Bertalda looked entreatingly at Undine, 'I have come to ask your forgiveness for my behaviour yesterday. I believe that you did indeed wish to give me joy by bringing my poor parents to the feast. O forgive me, forgive all the bold and unkind words I spoke, for indeed I am very unhappy.'

But the gentle Undine would let the miserable maiden say no more. She threw her arms around Bertalda's neck, and said, 'Bertalda, dear Bertalda, you shall live with me and be my sister. You shall come with me to Ringstetten this very day.'

The maiden dried her tears and looked timidly at the knight. He also felt sorry for Bertalda, nor did it please him to think of her venturing alone into the forest. Too well he knew the terrors which might surround her there. He took her hand, as he saw her timid look, and said in a gentle voice, 'You shall live with us at Ringstetten, and I and my wife will take care of you. But lest the good old fisherman is troubled as the days pass and you do not reach the cottage, I will send to tell him that you have come with us and are safe at Castle Ringstetten.' Then, giving Bertalda his arm, he placed her in the carriage with Undine. The knight himself mounted his horse and rode along gaily by their side, and soon they left the city and all sad thoughts behind.

At length, one fair summer evening, the travellers reached Ringstetten. There was much to make the knight busy after his long absence, and thus it was that Undine and Bertalda spent many days alone together. Often they would walk in the beautiful country which lay without the castle grounds.

One day, as they wandered along the banks of the river Danube, a tall man came toward them, and would have spoken to Undine. But Undine, gentle as were her ways, had no welcome for the stranger. When she saw him, a frown crossed her sweet face and she bid him at once begone. Shaking his head the tall man yet obeyed, and walking with hasty steps toward a little wood, he soon disappeared.

'Is not the stranger he who spoke to you in the city, the Master of the fountain?' cried Bertalda fearfully. She would always be afraid of the man who had told Undine the secret of her birth.

'Fear nothing, dear Bertalda,' said Undine hastily, 'the Master of the fountain shall not do you harm. I will tell you who he is, and then you will no longer be afraid. His name is Kühleborn and he is my uncle. It was he who carried you away from your mother's arms and put me there in your place.'

Then, as Bertalda listened with wide open eyes, Undine told her of her childhood's home in the crystal palace under the blue sea, and of the free and careless life she had lived in the cottage by the lake. She told her, too, of the coming of the knight, and of their wedding-day, when she had won for herself a soul, a gift given to no Undine save through the power of love.

Bertalda listened to the strange story in silence, but as she listened she felt a faint feeling of dread creep into her heart. And the feeling grew and grew until at last it seemed to stand as a wall between her and the gentle Undine.

At supper that evening she began to be sorry for the knight, who had married a lady beautiful indeed and good, yet one who seemed to belong to another world than theirs.

CHAPTER XII

CASTLE RINGSTETTEN

Now as the days passed, a change crept over those who dwelt in the castle.

Huldbrand saw that Bertalda seemed to shrink away from his beautiful wife. And when at length he asked her the reason that she no longer loved Undine so well as she had been used to do, she told him that she now knew from whence his wife had come. 'And for the spirit world,' said Bertalda, 'I do not care, for I know it not. It and those who have dwelt there fill me with fear and dread.'

Little by little the knight himself began to look at his wife with less loving eyes, little by little he began to shun her presence.

Then Undine, seeing that her husband's love grew less, wept, and the knight, seeing her tears, would speak kindly to her, yet even as he spoke he would leave her side to walk with Bertalda.

She, Bertalda, meanwhile grew once more rude and proud, nor could Undine's patience win her to behave more wisely.

Then in the long dark passages of the old castle, spectres began to appear to Huldbrand and Bertalda, and worse than any was the tall form of Kühleborn, or the Master of the fountain, as the maiden still called him.

Now one day, when Huldbrand had ridden to the hunt, Undine gathered all her servants together in the court of the castle and bade them bring a big stone to cover up the fountain which stood in the middle of the square.

The servants, who loved their mistress, hastened to obey her commands. A huge stone was carried into the court, and was just about to be placed on the fountain when Bertalda came hurriedly to the spot.

'The fountain must not be closed,' she cried haughtily, 'for it is from it that water is drawn for my daily bath.'

But Undine, who on other days had often given way to the wishes of Bertalda, was to-day determined that her will should be done.

'It is I who am mistress of the castle in the absence of my lord,' she said, and her voice was firm though it was kind, 'and the fountain shall be closed as I have commanded.'

'But look,' cried Bertalda angrily, 'the water itself bubbles and heaves as though disturbed at the thought of being shut out from the glad sunshine.'

The water was indeed, as the maiden said, fretting against the stones and throwing out sudden jets as though in a violent passion.

The more excited grew the water, however, the more determined grew Undine to have her order fulfilled, and that without delay.

As for the servants, they had no wish to please the haughty Bertalda, they were even glad to disobey her when that might be.

Accordingly they no longer delayed to do the will of their gentle mistress, and the stone was soon placed securely over the opening of the fountain. Undine then bent over it and silently wrote on the top of the stone some strange letters.

That evening, when Huldbrand came home, Bertalda met him with tears in her eyes, and complained to him of his wife's strange conduct.

'Tell me why you have ordered that the fountain should be sealed,' said the knight, turning sullenly to his wife. 'It was a strange deed.'

'I will tell you the reason when we are alone,' said Undine. 'It was a grave one indeed.'

'It matters not if Bertalda should hear,' said the knight, and he did not hide the impatience that he felt.

'I will tell you in her presence if you so desire,' said Undine, 'but I beseech you, desire it not.'

As the knight looked into her pleading face and let her sweet voice steal into his heart, he grew ashamed of himself. How could he ever be unkind to so fair, so good a wife!

Thinking thus Huldbrand did not speak, but he drew Undine gently from the room, that she might speak to him alone as she wished to do.

'Ah, now I can tell you,' said Undine, and she smiled in her content. 'You know that Kühleborn, my uncle, has begun to haunt the castle. I send him away in my displeasure, yet again and again he returns. Now I have shut the door by which he comes, and here he will disturb our peace no more. It is true that the stone can easily be raised by strong men, in spite of the letters which I wrote upon it. If you wish to do as Bertalda demands, remove the stone, yet do I warn you that Kühleborn may well harm the maiden, for against her he bears more ill-will than he does against others.'

Once more, as Huldbrand listened to his wife, he was ashamed. So gentle was she, so kind to the haughty maiden who but mocked at her for all her love. Peerless indeed was the soul of his beautiful wife, and once again love for her sprang up within his heart.

'The stone shall not be removed, nor shall anything that you order be undone, my sweet Undine,' said the knight.

At these words, and yet more at the kindness of his voice, Undine rejoiced. Then, seizing Huldbrand's hand, she begged him to grant her one request.

'If at any time, in the days that are to come,' she said, 'you upbraid me, promise that this you will never do while we are sailing or while we are near to sea or lake or tiny rivulet. For should one of my race hear you use harsh words toward me, then would they regain their power, and snatch me away from you for ever. Then would I be forced to dwell all the rest of my life in the crystal palace below the blue sea. Nor could I ever come up to you unless, indeed, I was sent by my kindred, when alas! only great sadness would befall us both. Promise me, therefore, that when we are near water, you will remember what I have now told you.'

Huldbrand promised, and hand in hand they went in search of Bertalda.

She meanwhile had called together some workmen, and as she saw the knight and Undine drawing near, she gave her orders to the men in a loud, discontented voice. 'The stone may now be removed. Hasten, see that it be done immediately!'

But the knight was angry with the maiden for daring thus to give what orders she pleased, and he shouted at once, so that the workmen might hear, 'The stone shall stay where it is! It shall not be removed!'

And the men went away, well pleased that they need not undo what their gentle mistress had ordered to be done.

Huldbrand then reproved Bertalda for her rude behaviour to his wife, but she scarcely heard his words, as she turned away in anger and hastened to her room.

Soon supper was placed on the table, but Huldbrand and Undine waited in vain for Bertalda. At length they sent a servant to call her, but the maid came back only to tell them that she was nowhere to be found. In her room, however, a letter had been left addressed to the knight. Huldbrand opened it hastily and read:—

'Forgive me, Sir Knight, that I have forgotten that I am only a poor fisher-girl. I will go to my father's miserable cottage, where I cannot well commit the same fault again. Fare you well, you and your beautiful wife.'

'You must go without delay to seek her and bring her back,' said Undine.

And Huldbrand did not need to be urged. Already he had ordered his horse to be saddled that he might ride after the maiden.

In vain he asked the servants in what direction Bertalda had gone. No one had seen her. It was only as the knight impatiently mounted his steed, that a page ran up to him crying, 'The lady Bertalda rode toward the Black Valley.'

Without a pause the knight darted off in the direction of the valley. He did not hear his wife's voice crying after him, 'Huldbrand, Huldbrand, go not there, not to the valley, Huldbrand, or, if go you must, take me, I entreat of you.'

Then when Undine saw that her cry was unheard, she ordered her palfrey to be saddled instantly, and mounting it, she rode forth alone to follow the knight into the Black Valley.

CHAPTER XIII

THE BLACK VALLEY

The Black Valley was a gloomy place. Fir-trees grew tall and dark on the banks of the stream, casting strange shadows on the sunny waters.

As the knight entered the valley, evening had fallen and the stream rushed, dark and sullen, between the rocks.

Huldbrand glanced anxiously from side to side, but no trace could be found of the maiden whom he sought. He began to fear lest already she were in peril, and thinking thus he urged his horse yet further into the valley.

Peering through the bushes as he rode, he at length caught sight of something white lying on the ground. Had he found Bertalda at last?

He spurred his horse onward toward the white gleam which had caught his eye, but the animal no sooner saw the object which had gladdened his master's eye than it started violently and refused to move. Then the knight dismounted, and tying his now rearing steed to an elm, he pushed his way on foot through the brushwood.

Thunder began to rumble around the mountains, and the evening dew fell cold and damp on the anxious knight.

He could still see the white figure lying on the ground, but as he drew nearer to it a strange dread struck at Huldbrand's heart.

'Was Bertalda asleep,' he wondered, 'or did she lie there unconscious, perchance even dead?'

He was close to her now, bending over her. She never stirred. He rustled the branches, rattled his sword. Still she lay there quiet, motionless. He called her by her name, 'Bertalda!' but no voice answered him. He called again, more loud, 'Bertalda!' but only a sorrowful echo answered his cry.

Then the knight bent nearer yet to the maiden, but darkness hid the face on which he longed to gaze.

Suddenly the whole valley was bright as at mid-day. A vivid flash of lightning showed to Huldbrand the face over which he bent.

It was a terrible face. And a voice, awful as the face, rang out harsh and hollow.

With a cry of terror the knight sprang away from the horrid vision. But was it a vision? Huldbrand knew that it was creeping after him, and he could catch some muttered words. 'Get you gone, get you gone,' he heard, 'there are evil spirits abroad. Get you gone, or I shall seize you and hold you fast,' and the white figure stretched out his bony arms to catch him. Ah! now the knight knew who it was that had given him so cruel a fright. It was none other than Kühleborn, the malicious water spirit.

Seizing his sword, Huldbrand struck fiercely at the white figure, only however to see it vanish, while a heavy shower of water drenched him from head to foot.

'He may wish to drive me away, but he shall not succeed in doing so,' murmured the knight. 'Bertalda shall not be left to the vengeance of this evil spirit.'

Huldbrand now turned back to go to his horse, but ere he reached the animal, he heard in the distance a sound of weeping. It reached his ears even though the thunder still rolled and the wind still blew. He hastened towards the spot from which the sound seemed to come. There, on the hillside, trying to climb up out of the darkness of the valley, he found Bertalda.

The maiden was too glad to see Huldbrand to remember how but lately he had angered her. She clung to him, calling him her deliverer, her knight, for to her too the valley had been full of horrible forms and strange visions.

Soothing her with kind words, Huldbrand led the maiden toward his horse.

But no sooner did the animal see his master approach with Bertalda on his arm than it began to rear, beating the air madly with its forefeet.

It was not possible to mount Bertalda, and the knight soon gave up the attempt. He drew the horse gently forward by the bridle, while with his other arm he supported the fearful maiden.

But Bertalda, though she was anxious to escape from the dark valley, could walk but slowly, and at each step her strength grew less. For Kühleborn had played her many pranks ere she had been found. The storm also had bruised her slender form.

At length she slipped from the knight's arm, and falling on the grass, she sighed, 'Leave me, noble knight, leave me to suffer the punishment I deserve.'

'I will never leave you, dear Bertalda,' cried the knight. As he spoke, the steed began to plunge even more furiously than before. It was impossible for Huldbrand to control the animal. All he could do was to force it away a few paces from where the maiden lay, for he feared lest the horse should trample her to death.

He had gone but a few steps when he heard her calling to him, 'Huldbrand, Huldbrand, leave me not alone,' for already all her courage had faded away.

As he hesitated, the knight heard the wheels of a wagon rumble slowly over the rough road that led through the valley. He at once called to the driver to come to his help. A man's voice called back quickly, 'Have but patience, and I will come.'

Soon afterwards Huldbrand saw two white horses appear through the trees. Then a wagon covered with a great white hood was to be seen, and last of all the driver, who was dressed in a white carter's frock.

The driver drew near to the knight and tried to help him to quiet his frightened steed.

'Do you know, Sir Knight, why your good horse shivers thus?' asked the carter, 'for if not I can tell you. A bad water spirit dwells in this valley, and often he would bewitch my horses when first I ventured through it. But now I have learned a little spell. If you wish it, I will whisper it in the ear of your steed, and he will stand steady as my greys.'

'You may try your spell,' said the knight, 'though I fear that it will be of but little use.'

Then the driver of the wagon went quietly up to the panting steed, and said a few words to it. At once the horse stood still, without a trace of the fear which had made it so restless and unmanageable.

Huldbrand had no time to wonder what the wagoner had said to his horse. He was too eager to get Bertalda out of the valley to think of anything else.

'My wagon will take the fair lady safely back to Ringstetten,' said the wagoner. 'She may sit in it in comfort, for it is filled with bags of the softest cotton.'

The knight was glad to accept this offer, and as his horse, though quiet, was tired and weary, Huldbrand himself was easily persuaded that he also should ride in the wagon with Bertalda, while his steed was fastened behind.

'It is well,' said the wagoner, 'that the road is downhill. My trusty greys will step out bravely.'

Thus they started, the driver walking by the side of his wagon.

And Bertalda and the knight did not heed the jolting of the wagon, as they sat side by side on the soft bags of cotton.

Suddenly they were startled by a loud shout from the driver.

'Steady, now, my trusty greys, steady, lest you fall.'

Already the wagon was in the midst of a stream of rushing water, and it seemed as though the horses must be carried off their feet. The wagoner had sprung into the wagon untouched by the swirling waters.

'This is a strange way by which to drive us,' said Huldbrand to the wagoner. 'It seems to go right into the middle of the stream.'

'Nay, now, Sir Knight,' laughed the driver, 'if you look again, you will see that it is the stream which is rushing across our path. See, it has overflowed its banks.'

The knight looked and saw that the whole valley was being rapidly flooded. Then, all at once, he knew that this was Kühleborn's doing.

'It is Kühleborn,' he cried aloud, 'Kühleborn the water spirit, who is doing his utmost to drown us. Do you not know a spell against his power?'

'Yea, by my troth I know a spell,' answered the wagoner, 'but ere I use it, I must tell you who I am.'

'I care not who you may be,' shouted the angry knight. 'See you not that there is no time to lose. The water is rising rapidly.'

'Nevertheless,' answered the man,' you shall hear my name, for I am Kühle-born!'

He laughed a mocking laugh, and at that moment the wagon seemed to disappear, and Bertalda and the knight were struggling in the flood. Above them rose the wagoner, who was indeed, as he had said, Kühleborn. Taller and taller he towered above them, until he seemed at last to change into a great white wave.

With horror-stricken eyes the maiden and the knight saw the wave swoop down upon the noble steed, which had been vainly struggling in the water. Then slowly once more the wave reared itself higher and higher yet above the heads of the two who watched and waited until they too should be for ever buried beneath the waters.

But ere the great white wave rolled down upon them, they were saved. Through the tumult of the waters a sweet voice floated to Bertalda and the knight. Then, as the moon broke through the clouds, they saw Undine on a hill looking down into the valley.

She rebuked the waters, she even threatened the vast wave that towered above Bertalda and the knight, until muttering gloomily it vanished from their sight.

As the waters ran more quietly through the valley, Undine flew to them swiftly as a bird and drew them up out of reach of the water. Bidding them rest a while, for they were weary, she went a little way off to fetch her white palfrey. Then, telling the knight to place Bertalda on the saddle, she led them safely back to the castle.

CHAPTER XIV

HULDBRAND FORGETS HIS PROMISE

Undine was full of joy when she had saved Bertalda and Huldbrand from the dangers of the Black Valley, and brought them back safely to Castle Ringstetten. Her joy grew daily greater as her husband became kind and gentle to her as he had used to be when they dwelt together in the cottage by the lake. Indeed the knight had grown ashamed of his careless words and ways. He would never again speak harshly to Undine or leave her side to spend long hours with Bertalda; so he thought to himself. For when she had hastened to save him and the maiden from the doom which had all but overtaken them, he had seen once more, in a flash, the soul of his beautiful young wife. It shone before him now, fair and spotless in its beauty.

Bertalda, too, had been touched by the goodness of her friend. She no longer wished to mock her gentle words, and though her heart was cold, she grew more humble.

Thus trouble and care passed away from Ringstetten, and spectres no longer haunted the dark corners of the castle.

Winter came, cold and chill, but it had no power to freeze the hearts of Undine and the knight.

Spring came, and the trees grew green, and the sky shone more blue, and the little birds began to use their wings. Soon the swallows and the storks came home from their long winter journeys. And those in the castle, as they thought of the fair countries these had seen, began themselves to wish to travel.

One beautiful evening Huldbrand with his wife and Bertalda walked along the banks of the river Danube. The knight, who had ofttimes sailed down the river, told them tales of the wonderful countries through which it flowed, and of the beautiful town of Vienna, which rose so proudly on its banks.

'Ah!' said Bertalda, 'how I wish we might sail to this city of which you tell.'

And Undine, ever anxious to give pleasure to her friend, said, 'Yes, let us visit Vienna while the spring is still fair.' Huldbrand also was pleased at the thought of the journey, only once he bent toward Undine and whispered, 'Kühleborn, will we not be in his power if we sail down the river?'

His beautiful wife only laughed. She was too happy now to fear her uncle's power.

They therefore got ready for the journey with much merriment and many hopes.

When at length the three travellers, with their attendants, set out on their voyage, it seemed as though all would be as joyful as they had wished. As they sailed on, the river grew more broad, more green the grasses too in the rich meadow-lands.

But erelong a shadow crept across their joy. The river, indeed, flowed smooth as before, the country smiled only more graciously upon the travellers, but Kühleborn had already begun to show that on this part of the river he could use his power.

Undine, it is true, reproved her uncle before he had done more than play a few tricks upon them. Yet though he would cease his pranks when she spoke, it was but a few moments before he was as troublesome as ever.

Soon the crew began to crowd together, whispering fearfully and glancing timidly at the knight and his fair ladies. Kühleborn was making them afraid.

Huldbrand saw their strange glances and he began to grow angry. He even muttered crossly, 'This is Undine's mad uncle come to disturb us. I would her strange kindred would leave us alone.'

Thinking thus, the knight looked with displeasure at his poor wife. She knew but too well what his glance meant, and worn out with sorrow and with her constant watch over Kühleborn, she at length fell fast asleep.

But no sooner were her eyes closed than her uncle again began his tiresome tricks.

It seemed to the sailors, and indeed to all on board, that they were bewitched, for look which way each one would, there before him, peering out of the water, was the head of a very ugly man.

Each man turned, in his terror, to point out to his fellow the hideous head. But on every face the same horror was already painted. Then when each tried to tell the other what each one had seen, they ended by crying out together, 'See, here is the face! nay, look, it is here!'

Undine awoke as the terrified crew broke into loud screams, and as she opened her eyes the ugly faces vanished.

But Huldbrand had not been frightened. He had been growing more and more angry, and now he would have spoken roughly to his wife, had she not pleaded with loving eyes and soft voice, 'For God's sake, rebuke me not while we are on the water. Bethink you of your promise.'

The knight was silent, for well he remembered how Undine had entreated him never to reprove her while she was near water.

Then she, seeing he was silent, whispered, 'Let us give up this voyage, for now has our joy turned into sadness. Let us go back to the castle where nothing can disturb us.'

Huldbrand, however, was not to be so easily restored to good humour. He answered her crossly, 'Why should I have to stay shut up at home? Even there can I have quiet only so long as the fountain remains sealed. I wish that your foolish kinsfolk—'

He could say no more, for Undine's hand was over his lips, and her voice was beseeching him to be silent.

Meanwhile Bertalda sat quietly in the ship, thinking of all the strange things that had happened. As she sat thus thinking, she unfastened a golden necklace which the knight had given to her, and holding it in her hand over the side of the bark she drew it carelessly through the water. Then dreamily she watched it as it gleamed and glistened in the light of the setting sun.

All at once a huge white hand came up out of the river, seized the necklace, and disappeared with it below the water.

Bertalda shrieked in terror, and a mocking laugh answered her cry.

Then could the anger of the knight no longer be concealed. He sprang up, shouting to the water spirits to claim no kinship with him, but to come and learn from his sword-thrusts how much he hated them.

The maiden meanwhile wept for her lost necklace. But Undine had thrust her hand into the water, and was murmuring strange words to herself, stopping from time to time to say to her husband, 'Chide me not here, Huldbrand, chide me not here, lest you lose me for ever.'

And, indeed, though the knight shook with rage, yet he spoke no word of reproach to his wife.

At length Undine drew out the hand which she had been holding under the water, and in it she held a coral necklace of wondrous beauty.

'Take it and weep no longer,' she said in her gentle voice, and she held the necklace out toward Bertalda. 'I have had it brought to me from the palaces below the sea. Grieve no longer for the one which you have lost.'

But the knight saw in the necklace only another sign of Undine's strange dealings with the water spirits. He sprang between Bertalda and his wife and snatched from Undine's hand the beautiful necklace, flinging it far away into the river. Then in his passion he turned to his wife, and cried, 'Go and abide with your kindred! You are a witch, go, dwell with those who are as you are, and take with you your gifts! Go, trouble us no more!'

Undine looked at Huldbrand. Tears were in her blue eyes, and she wept as a little blameless child might weep.

'Alas, beloved,' she sighed, 'farewell! No harm shall touch you while I have power to shield you from evil. Alas, alas! why have you sent me hence?'

She seemed to glide as she spoke over the edge of the bark, and be drawn down into the river. And the little waves lapped against the boat and seemed to sob as they whispered, 'Alas, alas!'

No sooner had the knight spoken than he knew what he had done. He had lost his wife, his beautiful fair-souled Undine. He lay on the deck stretching out empty arms, shedding bitter tears, until at length his misery made the strong man swoon.

THE LITTLE WAVES SEEMED TO SOB AS THEY WHISPERED,
'ALAS! ALAS!'

CHAPTER XV

HULDBRAND AND BERTALDA

When he recovered, the knight of Ringstetten went back to his castle with Bertalda. So bitterly did he mourn the loss of his gentle wife, that at length he began to believe that he would never cease to weep for her. Bertalda wept by his side, and for a long time they lived quietly together, thinking and talking of none save the beautiful Undine.

But as the months passed by, Huldbrand began to think a little less and yet a little less of his beautiful lost wife.

Now about this time the old fisherman appeared at the castle. He had come to tell the knight that it was time that his daughter Bertalda should come to live with him in his lonely cottage by the lake.

Then the knight began to think how strange and silent it would be in the castle if Bertalda left him. The more he thought about it the more he disliked the thought of being left alone.

At length he spoke to the fisherman and begged him not to take Bertalda away. 'Let her stay with me and be my wife,' said the knight.

And in time the fisherman yielded to the wishes of the knight, and the wedding-day was fixed.

Then a letter was sent to Father Heilman, begging him to come without delay to the castle that he might perform the wedding-rite between the knight and the lady Bertalda. Now Father Heilman was the very priest who had wedded Huldbrand to Undine in the cottage by the lake.

When the priest had read Huldbrand's letter he hastened at once to the castle.

Huldbrand and Bertalda were sitting side by side under the trees, the fisherman near them, when they saw the priest enter the court.

They all rose eagerly to welcome him, but Father Heilman began to speak without delay.

'Sir Knight, I have come with as great haste as my old limbs would carry me to tell you that I do not believe the beautiful Undine is dead. Last night and for many nights before, she was with me in my dreams, wringing her white hands, and crying, "Ah, holy Father, I live, I live. Let not Huldbrand forget me, for should he wed again great danger may, alas, come to him, nor will I have power to shield him. Help me, therefore, holy Father." What the dream meant I knew not until your letter reached me. Now have I come, not to marry you to Bertalda, but to tell you that Undine, your wife, is yet alive.'

The knight himself, as well as Bertalda and the fisherman, believed in their hearts that what the priest said was true, yet would they not own that they believed his words. Even the old fisherman, who so dearly loved his foster-child, thought that as the marriage with Bertalda had been arranged, it were well it should take place without more delay.

They all, therefore, refused to listen to the priest, when he reproached them for their conduct. They even told him, what was not really true, that they did not believe his foolish dreams.

Sadly shaking his head, the priest left the castle. He saw that should he speak again no one would listen to his words. Nor would he linger to taste any of the refreshments that were placed before him. He had failed to make any one believe his dream, and he was too sad to eat.

The following morning the knight sent to the nearest monastery for a priest, who promised to wed him to Bertalda in a few days.

CHAPTER XVI

BERTALDA'S WEDDING

The wedding-day dawned bright and clear, the guests assembled in the castle and wore their gayest garments, yet over everything there brooded a dark cloud. It seemed to the knight, as well as to his guests, that some one was missing from the feast, and the thoughts of all turned to the beautiful Undine.

The bride seemed happier than any one else, yet even she knew a cloud was in her sky.

Slowly the hours of the wedding-day dragged on, but at length the ceremony was over, the feast ended, and the guests ready to depart.

When they had gone, Bertalda, thinking to dispel the gloom which had now fallen upon her spirit, told her maids to spread out before her all her rich jewels and gorgeous robes. She would choose to-night the garments in which she would array herself on the morrow.

Her waiting-maids did as they were told, and when the dresses and jewels were spread out before their new mistress, they began to flatter her and tell her that none was fairer than she.

Bertalda listened with pleasure to their praises. Then looking at herself in the mirror she sighed. 'Alas, but see these little brown spots that have appeared on my neck.'

The maids saw indeed, as their mistress said, that there were freckles on her neck, but still they flattered her, saying that the little spots only made her skin look the whiter.

But Bertalda did not believe their words. She wanted to get rid of the freckles that had only lately appeared on her slender throat.

'Had I but water from the fountain, the spots would vanish in a day,' she cried pettishly.

Then one of Bertalda's maids thought to herself, 'My mistress shall have the water she so much desires,' and laughing gaily to herself, she slipped from the room.

In but a few moments heavy footsteps were heard in the court below. The footsteps tramped backward and forward.

Bertalda, looking from her window, smiled, for she saw that the noisy steps were those of workmen, who were busy removing the stone which had been placed over the fountain. She guessed that this was the doing of one of her maids, but she still smiled contentedly. The freckles would not spoil her beauty for another day. The water from the fountain would make them disappear, and that was all she cared about just then.

At first the workmen tried in vain to remove the stone. Perhaps some of them, remembering that their sweet young mistress Undine had ordered it to be placed there, did not try very hard to lift it from its place. All at once, however, the stone began to move. It almost seemed as though it were being pushed up from beneath. It moved slowly, then seemed to rise up into the air, after which it rolled on to the pavement with a tremendous crash.

Then slowly, slowly there rose out of the mouth of the well a white figure, veiled and weeping. And those who gazed spellbound at the sight saw that the figure which stepped from the fountain was that of a woman. Weeping and wringing her hands, she walked slowly, sorrowfully toward the castle.

The workmen now fled in terror from the court, while Bertalda with her maids still gazed from her window at the pale shadowy figure. As it passed beneath her window it looked upward, sobbing pitifully, and the bride saw under the veil the sweet sad face of the mistress of the castle, Undine.

Bertalda called aloud to her maids to go fetch the knight, her husband, but not one was found with courage to go in search of him.

On and on went the wanderer slowly, as though she would fain turn backward, on and up the stairs she knew so well, through the long quiet passages, and as she walked her tears fell yet more fast.

In a room at the end of the long passages stood the knight. A torch burnt dully by his side. As he stood there thinking of the days that had passed away for ever, he heard steps coming slowly along the passage. He listened, and, as he listened, the slow footsteps halted outside his door.

Soft fingers tapped, and then very gently the door was opened, and Huldbrand, standing before a long mirror, saw, without turning, a white-veiled figure enter and close the door.

'The stone has been taken away from the fountain, and I have come to you and you must die,' said a soft voice.

Ah, it was Undine, his beautiful lost Undine, who had come back to him. How he longed to see her face, yet how he feared to have the veil removed lest she should have changed since last he gazed upon her.

SLOWLY, SLOWLY THERE ROSE OUT OF THE MOUTH OF THE WELL A WHITE FIGURE

'If you are beauteous as in days gone by, if in your eyes I may see your soul tender as of old, draw aside your veil, that as I die I may gaze upon you,' faltered the knight.

Silently Undine threw back her veil, and Huldbrand saw her, fair as on the day he had won her for his bride. As he looked upon her, he knew that he had never loved any one in all the wide world as he loved Undine.

He bent toward the sweet face. Then Undine, kissing the knight, drew him into her arms and wept. And as she wept the tears flowed into his very heart and he also wept. Softly she laid him on his couch, and with her arms around him, Huldbrand died.

Then sorrowfully Undine raised herself from the couch, and sorrowfully she passed from the chamber.

'My tears fell on his heart until, for very sorrow, it broke,' she said, as she glided, a pale veiled figure, through the terrified servants.

And some who dared to follow her saw that she went slowly down toward the fountain.

CHAPTER XVII
THE BURIAL

Now when Father Heilman heard that the knight was dead, he hastened to the castle to comfort Bertalda. The priest, who but the day before had married the maiden to the knight, had already fled from the haunted house.

But Father Heilman found that the haughty spirit of the bride needed no comfort. She was more angry with Undine than sorrowful that she had lost the knight. Indeed, as she thought of the strange way in which Huldbrand had been snatched away from her, she cried aloud, 'Why did Huldbrand bring a water spirit to his home? She is worse than a mermaiden, she is a witch, a sorceress!'

Then the old fisherman, who heard her cruel words, hushed her, saying, 'It was God's will that Huldbrand should die, and Undine alone, forsaken, weeps for his death in great sorrow of soul.'

But if Father Heilman was not needed to comfort Bertalda, his presence was wanted at the burial of the knight.

Not far off there was a little village church to which the lord of Ringstetten and others of his race had given gifts. It was arranged that in the churchyard the knight should be laid to rest.

His shield and helmet were laid on his coffin and would be buried with him, for the knight of Ringstetten had left no son to bear them in the years that were to come.

On the day that had been fixed the mourners walked slowly toward the churchyard, Father Heilman in front carrying a crucifix.

Then slowly a figure clad in snow-white garments, and wringing her hands in great sorrow, came to join the mourners, who all wore black clothes as a sign of their grief. Those who noticed the white-veiled figure drew closer together, terror-stricken. Others, seeing them thus fearful, turned to see the reason of their fear, and soon these too drew aside, for the white-robed figure was in their very midst.

Seeing the confusion among the mourners, some soldiers, trying to be brave, as was their duty, spoke to the white-robed figure and even tried to drive her away. But she glided quickly past them and followed onward, still toward the little church.

The maids who were walking close to Bertalda saw that the white-veiled figure would soon be by their side, and they, lest she should harm them, drew back, so that it was easy for the shadowy form to keep close to the new-made bride.

Softly, noiselessly she moved, so noiselessly that Bertalda neither heard nor saw the phantom figure.

At length the mourners reached the churchyard and gathered around the grave. Then Bertalda, looking up, saw the white-veiled figure standing by her side, and knew that it was Undine.

Fear whispered to Bertalda to leave the veiled figure undisturbed, anger bade Bertalda order that it should at once depart. And anger was going to have its way, for Bertalda opened her lips to speak, but Undine shook her head and held out her hands as though she begged for mercy.

Then Bertalda remembered all the kindness Undine had shown toward her, and especially how lovingly she had held out to her the coral necklace as they were sailing on the Danube, and as she remembered her hard heart melted, and she wept.

At that moment Father Heilman began to pray, and all the mourners knelt around the grave, in which the coffin bearing the shield and helmet of the knight had now been placed.

When the prayer was ended the company arose, but the white-veiled figure was no longer to be seen.

Only on the spot where she had knelt a stream of crystal water gushed out of the earth. Quietly it flowed around the grave of the knight and then onward until it joined the river which ran past the little village church.

And in days to come the villagers would ofttimes point to the crystal stream as they told their children in solemn whispers that it, the little crystal stream, was none other than Undine, poor forsaken Undine, who thus surrounded and protected Huldbrand, her beloved.

Lector House believes that a society develops through a two-fold approach of continuous learning and adaptation, which is derived from the study of classic literary works spread across the historic timeline of literature records. Therefore, we aim at reviving, repairing and redeveloping all those inaccessible or damaged but historically as well as culturally important literature across subjects so that the future generations may have an opportunity to study and learn from past works to embark upon a journey of creating a better future.

This book is a result of an effort made by Lector House towards making a contribution to the preservation and repair of original ancient works which might hold historical significance to the approach of continuous learning across subjects.

HAPPY READING & LEARNING!

LECTOR HOUSE LLP
E-MAIL: lectorpublishing@gmail.com